MIDNIGHT ICE

A Madison Night Mystery

Diane Vallere

POLYESTER PRESS BOOKS | Los Angeles, CA

To Doris Day

INTRODUCTION

In the not-so-distant past, a major storm, coupled with a computer glitch, stranded thousands of passengers at the Dallas/Fort Worth airport. As the passengers searched for their mislabeled luggage and scrambled for new flight connections, three lives intersected thanks to identical vintage suitcases.

This is the story of what happened when one woman with a knack for solving mysteries picked up the wrong bag.

ONE

I started my getaway on the floor. And by floor, I mean the beige speckled linoleum tile squares that covered the ground by the Monterey Airport baggage claim. A fragile-looking Chihuahua broke free from the grasp of a young girl and ran over to sniff me. The girl moved toward the dog but her dad held her hand tightly. She started to cry. I tried to roll over again, but a stab of pain shot through my knee cap and I flopped back onto my butt. My face flushed with embarrassment, not over the fact that a group of official looking men and a steady stream of travelers had seen the turquoise cotton panties I wore under my early sixties aqua sheath dress but because I knew I needed to ask someone for help getting back up and I didn't like to ask for help strangers, official-looking or otherwise.

The passengers around me gave me a one-foot berth, enough to indicate I was woman down, but not enough to give up their prime spot for retrieving their luggage as it came off the beltline.

A man in a black suit approached me. He corralled my crutches to the side with his foot, then stood behind me and put his hands under my arms. I held the end to the Chihuahua's leash in my hand as I stood, then crutched to the little girl, her dog trailing behind me, and returned her charge. The official-looking man stood by the luggage conveyor belt watching me.

"You okay?" asked the man who had helped me up. Now that we were face to face I noticed he was not much taller than I was. He was tan, with a mole under his left eye. His longish sandy-blond hair was parted on the side and tucked behind his ears. He held a piece of paper that said Day.

"Reservation for Day? That's me. Give me a second to get my suitcase and we can go."

The crowd of travelers had thinned significantly, and only a few bags were left on the luggage belt. My blue and white 1950's hardback suitcase was one of them. I anchored the crutches under my arms and moved closer to the belt. It didn't take a rocket scientist to realize I couldn't pick up my suitcase while balanced on the crutches.

"Which one's yours?"

"The blue and white one," I answered.

He pulled the suitcase from the conveyor belt and turned away from me. He walked fast, faster than I would have expected considering he was well aware of my crutch-handicap, I didn't ask him to slow down. I was going to function the way I always functioned, post-knee injury or no post-knee injury.

The driver and I reached the parking lot within twenty seconds of each other. When I arrived at the car he was shutting the trunk with my luggage inside. He opened the back door of the sedan and waved for me to go inside.

"Ms. Day," he said with a nod.

"Actually, it's not Day, it's Night." His eyebrows and his mouth turned down at the same time, as if little puppet strings from somewhere below us controlled is expression. "Madison Night," I added, turning my introduction into a James Bond-ism.

"Madison Night?" he checked his clipboard. "I have a reservation for D. Day."

"I didn't want to travel under my own name. If you check your paperwork, you'll find my name matches the name on the credit card used to hold the reservation." His suspicion was obvious, but I ignored it. My knee throbbed from the fall by the baggage claim and now, to add insult to injury, my underarms ached from the speed-crutching I'd done to keep up with him.

I pulled the crutches out from under me and pushed them into the back seat, then followed them into the dark black interior. I slid my license and credit card from the wallet inside the quilted leather bag I had slung across my body and waited for the inevitable request to see them. Instead, he shut my door and walked around the other side, then climbed in behind the wheel.

"Forgive me, Ms. Night. When I saw a reservation for

D. Day, going to Carmel By-The-Sea, well, I thought I might be having a brush with fame."

"To tell you the truth, Doris Day is why I'm going to Carmel. She's like a—" I stopped talking abruptly, realizing I didn't know how to finish the sentence to a stranger.

"You know her?" he asked.

"She's kind of like a Godmother."

"I guess I am having that brush with fame. Doris Day's Goddaughter."

I knew right then and there I should have corrected him, let him know I didn't really know Doris Day. That if she was like a godmother, it was of the fairy Godmother type. Ever since I'd learned of her in my teenage years, after discovering we shared the birthday of April third, I'd developed more than a passing interest in the actress, copying her look, her style, and most of all, her integrity. It was that bubbly personality that had carried her through so many tragedies in her own life that I responded to, that I used as a guide for how to live my own life. When I'd gotten out of the hospital in Pennsylvania, knowing I was alone in my recovery, I knew there was one place I could go to restore my emotional strength and start to move on.

Cypress Inn, Doris Day's hotel in Carmel By-The-Sea.

I'd booked the reservation while on my way to the Philadelphia airport. My timing, though spontaneous, was perfect. The hotel was under renovation, so it would be ready for the annual art festival in a few months. Something about the renovation rang a bell with me, but I didn't know what. I'd read off my credit card number to hold a room, then sat back and tried to forget why I wanted to get away.

We arrived at the hotel twenty minutes later. Traces of the pain killer I'd taken between flights at the Dallas airport were still in my system and the grogginess hadn't yet worn off. I was eager to get to my room and finally relax.

I checked in relatively quickly while a porter stood nearby, waiting for my room number to be assigned so he could deliver my bag. Posters from Doris Day movies lined the walls of the concierge desk and the small reception area. Two chubby ladies in pastel linen suits walked behind me, both led by dogs on leashes. The woman in the lilac wore a matching hat with a bit of netting over her face. Her dog, a Yorkie, pranced next to a white Peek-a-poo who belonged to the woman in sea-foam green. Nearby, a cat was curled up on a floral sofa, napping in a spot of sunshine.

"Ms. Night, your room is 319," said the handsome concierge. A plastic nametag reading Harrison was pinned to the lapel of his light tan suit. He had salt and pepper hair that looked as if it had been recently cut, revealing a small border of untanned skin by his hairline. If he were the sort to dye his hair he would have looked younger, but I immediately liked that he wasn't and didn't. "Lionel will take your luggage to your room for you. We have sherry at four every afternoon in the lounge, jazz in the courtyard from seven to ten, and Terry's Lounge is open until eleven for dinner, or drinks if you fancy a nightcap."

"Thank you," I said to Harrison. Lionel went one direction with my suitcase and I went the other.

The elevator lobby was at the end of a small carpeted hallway that ran past the restaurant. A large mirror hung on the wall above a marble table with a hotel phone and an ugly, squat, adobe-colored lamp that failed to complement the hotel's mid-century modern décor. The lamp hadn't been turned on and the small waiting area was dark.

I felt for the knob on the lamp and clicked it repeatedly but nothing happened.

Voices from men waiting for their elevator floated to me from around the corner. They seemed not to notice my presence.

"She's here. I haven't seen her yet, but she's here. The message said she'd be available tonight, after ten," said the shorter man.

"Is that when you're going to see her?" asked the man in the suit. "And what about the last guy? Is he showing up to make sure she's in good hands?"

"I hope so. I've been waiting a long time. I hope she's as pretty as she sounds."

I crept forward and looked at the men. The taller one was in a Gray suit with a white shirt unbuttoned at the neck. He wore glasses without the rims, and smelled like expensive aftershave. The other man, shorter but more muscular, had on a striped shirt and tie under his sport coat and blue jeans.

I tried to pretend I wasn't listening in on their conversation, considering they didn't know I was standing there. I half-turned, thought about stepping back into the shadows until after they'd gotten on the elevator, but that's when they spotted me.

Gray suit nodded his head at me. "I bet that sounded funny to you, ma'am," he said.

"To be honest, I wasn't paying attention. I'm a little lost in my thoughts," I lied.

"First time in Carmel?" asked Blue Jeans.

"Yes."

"You picked a nice hotel. Doris Day's hotel, but by the looks of you, I'm betting you already knew that."

I looked past the men to my reflection in a decorative mirror. He was right. In my vintage aqua double-knit sheath dress and coordinating ivory jacket lined in matching aqua silk, I looked like an Avon Lady from the early sixties, not the carefree vacationer I was trying to be. But this was how I was comfortable, in my vintage ensembles. Drop me in a mall and I'd have a panic attack trying to put together the kind of outfit that might be featured in a recent fashion magazine.

I ran my fingers through my short blond hair, trying to bring back the pouf that I'd started with before I'd caught the plane in Dallas. "Your bet would have paid off. I've been a fan of hers my whole life."

"A fan? I would have guessed you're related. You look just like she looks on that poster." He pointed to the *Lover Come Back* poster on the wall. "Minus the silly hat."

The men laughed.

I could have introduced myself. I could have elaborated on Doris Day as style icon. I could have told him I owned that very hat. Instead, when the bell to the elevator chimed, I maneuvered my way inside.

The two men followed.

"What floor?"

"Three," I said. I didn't know whether it was the way I'd left Pennsylvania, like I was running from someone or something, or the fact that Gray suit didn't hit another floor's button after he hit the three, that put me on alert.

When the car arrived on the third floor, both men stepped out. Maybe we were all on the third floor, I thought. But when they let me pass them, I knew I was being watched, and I didn't like the feeling. About ten feet down the hall I stopped to study the plastic signs that indicated which room was where, then went the direction opposite 319. The elevator door was still open, but the men weren't in the hallway. I couldn't control the sound of the crutches even though I was on carpet. Plunk, creak, step. Plunk, creak step. As I passed the elevator, I looked inside. The two men stood there, blue jeans on his cell phone. Gray suit smiled at me.

"I got turned around, I guess."

"Happens to me all the time," he replied.

I couldn't be sure, but it seemed like he took his finger off the button and the doors slid shut. I rounded the corner and leaned against the wall, counting silently to myself, waiting to see if the doors would reopen. They didn't.

In a matter of minutes, I arrived at my room. The suitcase sat on a luggage cart by the end of my bed. The sun filtered through the sheer white curtains and I could see the water from my window. I'd requested a room with a view and this room didn't disappoint. I wanted to shower, to change clothes, and to relax on my balcony with a glass of wine from a local vineyard. I wanted to start to forget.

I undid the brass clamps on the suitcase and flipped it open. And that's when I realized I had a whole other set of problems.

TWO

"This is Madison Night in room 319. I just checked in. The wrong suitcase was delivered to my room. Yes, I can hold." I sat on the bed and stared at the neatly folded contents of the suitcase. And by neatly folded, I meant obsessively neat. I knew my spontaneous decision to get out of town had left me packing in a less than orderly fashion, but even if I'd been planning this getaway for a month I would never have packed like this.

While I waited for the concierge to locate Lionel and figure out where my suitcase had gone, I stared at the top layer of the suitcase interior. It was covered in Ziploc baggies, each labeled and numbered. I recognized hair products, cosmetics, and lotions all packed individually. Why would a person separate their toiletries, especially if they checked their luggage? Why use the Ziploc bag at all if you didn't have to go through the security screening with liquids?

"Ms. Night?" said the concierge, returning to the phone.

"Yes?"

"Lionel says that's your bag."

"That is most definitely not my bag," I said.

"Would you like to come down to the lobby and talk to him?"

"I'm on my way."

I left the suitcase open and slipped my feet back into my white sneakers. My underarms were sore from the crutches rubbing the double-knit polyester dress against my skin. I limped a few steps, favoring my injured knee, to test if I could make the trip without the cursed wooden instruments, but it seemed, if I wanted to be mobile, I had no other choice.

Lionel was waiting for me by the concierge desk. The man who had checked me in waved me over. "Ms. Night, I'm sorry for any inconvenience, but Lionel assures me he took your suitcase directly to your room. Isn't that right, Lionel?"

"Yes, ma'am. I noticed the tags on it. I moved here from Dallas, so I was thinking I'd like to ask you what part you're from. You did come from Dallas, didn't you?"

"I connected through Dallas, but I'm not from there. I live in Pennsylvania." Live. Lived. Once lived. I didn't bother explaining my issues with tense or my own question as to whether or not I'd go back.

"Did you check the luggage tag, Ms. Night?"

"No, I'm afraid I didn't. I opened the suitcase and the contents were unfamiliar."

The two men looked at each other. "Would you like us to call the airport for you?" the concierge asked.

"No, I can do that, and I should probably have the tag in front of me when I do so. I'm sorry for the confusion. Good night, gentlemen."

I turned around and went back the direction from which I'd come, back to my room, back to the awesome view and the wrong suitcase. I sat on the bed, then fell backward and spread my arms out to my sides and stared at the ceiling.

I wanted to wash off the day. I limped to the bathroom, where an assortment of shampoo, conditioner, lotion, and soap, but most of all, a post-shower plush white terrycloth robe awaited me. After stripping down to nothing, I stepped in under a hot spray of water, where I stood for the better part of an hour.

I towel-dried and belted myself into the robe, then emerged from the cocoon of steam into my room. The sun was setting, a glow of purple and orange in the sky above the mountainous horizon and deep blue water. I found the mini-bar and poured myself a glass of Sauvignon Blanc, then opened the doors and stood on my balcony. The breeze was cool against my skin. I drank in the air coming off the water, the lingering scent of honeysuckle and grass. This was heaven. This was the most beautiful view I'd seen. No wonder Doris Day had chosen to live here.

I sipped my wine and leaned on the white metal banister. Couples dotted the street, sprinkled with children and dogs. This was a walking town and I was barely able to walk. Not for the first time, I cursed Brad. I cursed the way he'd ended it, two weeks after telling me, one romantic night in the back of Pierot's interior design studio, he wanted us to be together forever. I cursed how I'd skied away from him after he told me he was already married; I cursed the accident that had sent me to the hospital.

A part of me still didn't believe it was over, even if I knew it had to be. That's why I'd left Pennsylvania with a quickly packed suitcase for a spontaneous trip to Carmel, California. I had to go someplace where I knew I wouldn't see him, because the longer I stayed in Pennsylvania, the more I thought I saw him everywhere I went. And the longer I went without running into him, the stronger that feeling became, the feeling I was being watched, that he was there, but not there. I didn't know if it was wishful thinking or paranoia, but I knew I had to get away.

Deep voices pulled me away from the memory of the accident. I looked around, at the balcony to my left and to my right. Both were vacant. The creaking above me let me know my company was one floor up. I sipped the wine and listened to the snippets of conversation.

"The only thing I know is she was supposed to arrive today and we'll see her tonight."

"Do you trust your source?"

"I don't see any choice right now."

"So she's at the hotel. She could be here already. She could be in any one of these rooms and we wouldn't even know it."

"Yeah. We might have walked right past her and not even known. Do you know who brought her?"

There was no answer.

"Doesn't matter. She's going to be in the bar tonight, and that's when we'll grab her."

Grab her. A chill ran down my spine.

"You don't think anybody will notice you grabbing a blonde from the bar?"

"I can't see any other choices." There was a pause. By now I'd identified the voices as the two men from the elevator. "So here's the plan. Get into disguise by nine, meet at the bar at nine-thirty. When she shows up, we hit it and quit it. Until then, it's the friendly stranger routine. got it?"

The friendly stranger routine. That's what I'd allowed myself to believe only moments earlier. I gripped the metal banister harder for balance.

"Hey Louis, did you find out where she's coming from?"

"Someplace on the east coast. I don't know the details, but I know she made a stopover in Dallas."

That's when I dropped the glass.

THREE

"What was that?" asked one of the voices.

I stumbled backward, through the balcony doors. My right hand grabbed at the sheer curtains that blew in and out of the room, steadying myself. I was afraid to be visible. I slid the glass door shut and pulled the cord that blocked the sunlight from the room. I lowered myself to the floor next to the plush Queen Anne chair in the corner.

Minutes later there was a knock on my door. I tried to curl into a ball but my injured knee wouldn't bend. I twisted to my side and lay down against the carpet. The slightest task of breathing in, breathing out, was too loud and threatened to give away my presence.

The knocking started up again. "Ms. Night? This is Jack Jordan, hotel security. I'm here to check on your luggage. Ms. Night, are you in there?"

I wanted to get up, to open the door, to tell this Jack Jordan there were men in the room above me who wanted to grab me at the stroke of ten o'clock, but even as I thought the words, I knew I would sound crazy. There had to be another explanation.

"Ms. Night?" he repeated.

Stop saying my name! I screamed internally. Out loud, I said nothing.

A piece of white paper slipped under my door. I sat on the floor by the arm chair for another two minutes, marked off by the red neon clock that sat on the nightstand next to the bed. Finally, I pushed myself up and retrieved the paper. It was on hotel letterhead.

DEAR MS. NIGHT,

WE'VE BEEN NOTIFIED of a luggage mix-up at DFW airport thanks to a storm that knocked out their computers. We have no word on where your luggage is or how soon we can get it to you, but we hope to have an answer shortly. In the meantime, please contact our front desk for any toiletries or immediate needs you might discover, and we will do our best to accommodate you.

SINCERELY,
Jack Jordan
Manager, Hotel Security

. . .

I MOVED to the hotel phone and dialed the operator, then asked to be connected to my airline. I met with a recording that acknowledged an unusually long hold time and issued a blanket apology to callers concerned with missing luggage. I held for a half a minute more, then hung up.

Within seconds, the phone rang. "Hello?" I answered.

"Is this Ms. Night in room 319?" said a male voice.

I slammed the phone onto the receiver before contemplating my very actions confirmed who I was. Before the phone could ring again, I called the front desk.

"This is Madison Night. Would it be possible for me to change rooms?"

"Is there a problem with your room?" asked Harrison. "You requested a view and we think you have one of the most spectacular that we have to offer."

"I know, yes, that's true." I looked at the crutches lying across the bed. "I was wondering if you had anything closer to the first floor. I didn't expect to have such trouble with the crutches."

"Would you like to use our hotel wheelchair?"

"No!" I answered quickly. "Is there a Jack Jordan who works for the hotel?"

"Yes," he paused. "He's our security manager. Ms. Night, are you sure there's no problem?"

"Can you ask Mr. Jordan to meet me in the bar at nine o'clock this evening?"

"Mr. Jordan is not in the habit of meeting guests for drinks."

"Tell him—tell him I've been hired to investigate this hotel. Tell him Ms. Day asked me to meet with him."

The concierge's voice dropped to whisper. "Ms. Day arranged this?"

"Yes," I lied.

"I'll deliver the message."

I hung up the phone. Now what? I'd demanded a meeting with the head of security, who I didn't know, who wouldn't recognize me. Or maybe he would. Maybe he was one of the voices from the balcony above me. Maybe he was planning to grab me. Maybe I'd just organized a meeting with the man who I wanted to avoid.

Or maybe I was going crazy.

It was after seven and I was still in the hotel bathrobe. I had nothing to wear except for the vintage blue and white double-knit polyester dress and jacket I'd worn on the plane, and even though I was most comfortable in my sixties vintage attire, right now, that outfit felt too conspicuous. I looked at the suitcase sitting on the luggage cart. No, those were someone else's things. I wouldn't want a stranger rooting around through my things, and I was willing to bet the obsessive-compulsive who had packed three different sizes of hand sanitizer in separate Ziploc baggies wanted it even less.

I redressed in my sheath dress and used the hotel hair drier to fluff my short blond hair into its normal bubble style, draped my small handbag over my shoulder, and left with the crutches digging into my underarms.

Two blocks from the hotel I found a souvenir store. I bought two packs of cotton panties, an elastic bandage, and a navy blue sweatshirt with Carmel embroidered across the chest in gold and white thread. I asked the saleslady to cut the tags from the sweatshirt so I could put it on immediately. I added a pair of sunglasses from the display rack, a travel-sized tube of Motrin, and a pink lip-gloss, paid, and left. The short man from the elevator stood in front of the store, his back to me.

"I don't know if she arrived or not. She was due today, but there was some kind of mix-up in Dallas," he said into a cell phone.

A shiver ran down my spine despite the warmth of the sweatshirt. The man turned around and saw me, then smiled and pulled his phone away from his head.

"Hey, it's the pretty little blonde from the elevators. You find your room okay?" he asked.

"Yes, I did."

"That's too bad. My friend and I were trying to figure out which one of us would have the honor of helping you." He reached out and grabbed for my plastic shopping bag. "But my friend isn't here now, so I guess the honor's all mine. Call me Louis."

"I'm not done shopping yet," I said instead of offering a return introduction. I held the bag even though he tried to pull it from my grasp.

"Maybe you're not, but the stores are. It's closing time around here."

I looked behind me. On the other side of the window, the clerk turned the Open sign to Closed. The lights were out in the store next to them. I tugged on the shopping bag, trying to break it free from his grasp. One of the handles broke. The bag dropped and split, my personal items spilling onto the sidewalk around the feet of people swirling around us.

Louis stared at the oversized sunglasses, anti-inflammatories, and cotton panties. He made no move to pick any of it up. Slowly, he looked up at me. His cheeks were taut, his lips drawn.

I couldn't read his eyes because they were hidden behind his own pair of sunglasses, but I imagined they weren't smiling.

"Kind of suspicious, taking a getaway and not packing your essentials. By the looks of it, you didn't plan on this vacation."

"Is this man bothering you?" said another man, approaching us.

It took me a second to recognize Harrison the Concierge without his hotel uniform, but when I did, I could have hugged him if it wouldn't have included falling off the crutches.

Louis backed away from us and held his hands in the air. "I was just offering to help, that's all." Before either one of us could say another word, he turned around and disappeared into the crowd of swirling people.

FOUR

Harrison corralled my purchases, hugged them to his chest, and stood. I leaned on the crutches and reached for the items, but he took the torn bag from me instead, loaded everything back inside, and knotted the handles together.

"Are you okay?" he asked.

"I'm fine. I didn't expect that man to—to—"

I didn't know what it was I'd expected or not expected from the man who called himself Louis. I didn't know how to explain to Harrison that I'd overheard very strange things. And I didn't know how to rationalize, to myself, that little by little, I was losing touch with reality.

"You seem a little shaken up. Would you like me to walk you back to the hotel?" Harrison asked.

I scanned the street, looking for signs of Louis, but there were none. I didn't know where he had gone. I wanted to take Harrison up on his offer, but I didn't know how to explain my paranoia without looking like a fool.

"Only if I can buy you a drink to say thank you."

Harrison looked surprised. "I thought you wanted to have a drink with our security manager?"

"Yes, that's true."

I thought for a moment and bit my lip. "I'm sorry. Is there another way I can say thank you?"

He blushed, and then I blushed, realizing how the whole thing had sounded. First I'd come off like I was trying to fill my happy hour dance card, and now I sounded like a cougar on vacation.

We walked to the hotel side by side, me on the crutches and Harrison holding my bag. I wanted nothing more than to throw the crutches away, to burn them, to wake up tomorrow morning and be able to walk like I walked before the skiing accident, but the voice of the hospital doctor echoed in my head. *Recovery will take time. Don't try to rush it.*

We reached the hotel quickly. I leveraged my weight against the banister and hopped up the three steps in front of the hotel door. I turned to face Harrison and looped my hand through the handle of the shopping bag.

"Thank you," I said. "I'm sorry I already made other arrangements for tonight."

"Tell you what. I'll come to the bar around nine. If you're alone, I'll join you. If you're with Mr. Jordan, I won't."

"That hardly seems fair. You're helping me and now I'm inconveniencing you."

"Ms. Night, I'm happy to help you. In fact, if there's anything you need, anything you forgot to buy at that drug store, I want you to call me." He pulled a small notepad out of his jacket pocket and wrote a phone number on a blank piece of paper, then tore it off and handed it to me.

"Does the hotel offer this kind of service to every guest?" I asked.

He leaned in and whispered, "Only the ones who know Ms. Day." When he pulled back, he smiled a warm smile.

It was well after eight by the time I returned to my room. I hadn't seen any other familiar faces in the lobby or hallway, and I hoped the opposite was true as well. In less than an hour I'd be sitting with the hotel security manager and I'd be able to tell him about the conversation I'd overheard. If he believed me, I'd tell him about the men by the elevators. Harrison could verify one of the guests had approached me on the street. I felt better knowing I was doing something about the situation, versus locking myself in my room and fearing for the worst. The only thing I did fear was being recognized. Walking around in a vintage dress with a sixties-style blond bubble cut wasn't doing me any favors in the anonymity category, and my one attempt to blend in, in the Carmel sweatshirt, had already been made. I needed some kind of disguise, but aside from wearing the hotel bathrobe, I had no other options.

Unless…the suitcase. Maybe there was something in the suitcase.

I flipped it open and dug past the layer of Ziploc baggies to the neat piles of folded clothes. I set the baggies on the bed, exposing a red and white bandana print and a cowboy hat. What the—?

I closed the suitcase and located a luggage tag right next

to the white tag the airline had wrapped around the handle. "Elliott Lisbon" read the name. Elliott. This was one odd dude. What kind of a weekend did he think he was taking? A country and western escape?

I moved the cowboy hat to the side and picked up the red and white bandana print. It was a long prairie skirt, the kind I passed over in countless thrift shops while I looked for the sixties vintage I favored, only, this one had tags attached. Was Elliott a cross-dresser? I put the skirt back into the suitcase and rooted further down. A red and white poppy print peeked out from below something chambray. It was a swing dress with dark brown accents. I could wear that, I supposed. Whoever this Elliott character was, he was nothing like me, and that might work to my advantage.

I changed into a clean pair of panties and pulled the swing dress over my head. It was pretty in a sundress kind of way. Repeated washings would soften the fabric, but like the bandana skirt, this dress had tags on it, too. I imagined Elliott shopping for this weekend with the same care with which he had packed his toiletries. I imagined, for a second, the stranger's reaction when he opened my suitcase and saw my polyester dresses and four tubes of sunscreen. I was sure it would be a letdown.

I fished the elastic bandage out of the bag from the drug store and wound it around my knee, tight enough to minimize the swelling but not so tight I cut off my circulation. I swallowed four anti-inflammatories with a glass of water from the sink and looked at my reflection.

Exhaustion painted the two dark circles under my eyes.

I needed to sleep tonight. The time change, going from the east coast to the west coast, had left me feeling like it was going on midnight, not nine. And being a morning person, I wasn't used to being up until midnight. I'd make my meeting with Mr. Jordan brief. I'd tell him what was going on and I'd retire.

I ran cool water into my hands and ran my hands through my hair, then massaged a dollop of complimentary hotel moisturizer into it and combed it straight back. My lips were rosy, as were my cheeks. As the clock approached nine, I thrust my room key into my handbag, grabbed the crutches, and headed down to the bar.

I took a seat along the wall next to the fireplace and looked for familiar faces. I saw none. A cocktail waitress approached me and I ordered a glass of white wine. As she left to fill my order, I saw my worst nightmare, standing in the entranceway. The two men from the elevator, engrossed in a heated conversation with Harrison the Concierge. With them was a fourth person, and there was no mistaking his identity.

It was my Ex, Brad Turlington.

FIVE

Brad had followed me from Pennsylvania. My paranoia had been on target.

I slouched down in my chair and watched the scene. From my vantage point, which was across a crowded room where people and pets mingled over wine and cheese, I knew I wouldn't hear their conversation, so I listened to their body language. From what it was telling me, these four men were arguing.

Harrison was doing the talking and the other men were listening. His gestures, though kept close to his body, were emphatic.

Louis was red in the face. He didn't like what he was being told.

And then there was Brad. He wore a straw Homburg tipped down low over his forehead. His wavy black hair peeked out in the back. He stood inches over the other men, his white zip front GE nylon windbreaker open over an orange and white checkered shirt. His hands were in the pockets of his khaki trousers, and the sunlight gleamed off of the face of his 1960's Rolex Submariner watch. I knew the watch. I'd given it to him for Christmas less than a year ago.

I felt sick. My heart raced and I shifted to the side, to remain in the shadow of the fireplace. It couldn't be, it couldn't be! I was trapped in a nightmare of past and present. I wanted to leave but standing up and fussing with the crutches would only draw attention to me, attention I couldn't afford.

The fourth man, the one in the suit, had his arms crossed over his chest. His attention was so focused on Harrison's face he didn't notice the small dog sniffing his shoe. Suddenly, as if startled, he kicked his foot out with a jerk. The dog jumped backward. A woman in a navy blue dress scooped up the dog and glared at the man. After he apologized to her, his eyes swept the room. I lowered my head and slunk down further.

A cocktail waitress came around to check on different tables and, when she got close enough to block my view of the men, I waved her over.

"Hi, I'm supposed to be meeting someone here, but I need to leave," I whispered. "Would it be possible to leave a message with you?"

"Sure," she said, her hand fishing through the pocket of a faded blue floral apron tied around her waist.

She handed me a ballpoint pen and a blank order ticket. Hastily I scribbled on it. *Mr. Jordan. I couldn't wait. Please meet me tomorrow morning for breakfast. Madison Night (room*

319). I folded the paper and wrote "Jack Jordan, Hotel Security" on the more blank of the two sides of the paper. I held it out to her and she took it.

"Are you okay? You look like you saw a ghost."

"Worse than a ghost, I think. Is there a way out of here other than the entrance past the bar?"

She looked over her shoulder. I followed her gaze. The men were gone and I didn't know which direction they'd headed.

"There's the service elevator off the kitchen, but I can't let you take it."

"Please," I said. I reached out and put my hand on her forearm. She looked at it, then back at me.

"Are you sure you're okay?" she asked again.

My mind scrambled for something to say without sounding crazy. "I'm sorry. I'm on a bit of medication from an injury last week and I feel woozy. I should get back to my room."

"Let me get someone from the hotel to escort you back to your room."

"Wait, do you have a wheelchair?" I asked.

"Yes."

Before I could stop her, she left.

I knew I wasn't woozy from medication. Aside from the jetlag, my mind was clear. I looked around the room again and picked out Louis, Brad, and Gray Suit at the bar, their backs to me. I wasn't sure where Harrison the Concierge had gone, but this was as good a chance as any for me to get out of there. I stood up and reached for the crutches, then headed past the other guests toward the kitchen. A collapsible wheelchair sat against the wall. I looked through the glass on one of the doors and saw the cocktail waitress talking to Harrison.

I put my head down and left the way I'd come. I reached my room undetected. I threw the crutches on the carpet and sat on the bed. I needed to talk to someone. I needed to find out what was going on. I needed an ally.

I dialed the operator. "Hello, this is Madison Night in room 319. I'm trying to reach Jack Jordan from hotel security. Is there a way to reach him?"

"Hold for a moment and I'll ring the concierge desk," she said politely.

"No!" I answered quickly. "Please don't. Is there a way to get a message to him directly, without involving anyone else from the hotel?"

"I can page him to call me. What would you like the message to be?"

"Tell him I'm sorry I had to cancel—no. Tell him I need to see him—no, not that either. Can you tell him to call me?" I held my breath, knowing how I sounded. "It's in regards to an issue with the hotel."

"Ms. Night, if your room is somehow unsatisfactory, I can try to make different arrangements for you."

"No, that's not it. There's something going on tonight he needs to know about."

"Ms. Night, are you in some kind of trouble?" she asked.

"Please page Mr. Jordan. I'll be in my room waiting for his call."

My knee throbbed. I leaned back on my tush and spun until I was long ways on the bed. My foot kicked the suitcase balanced on the luggage rack by the end, and the case tipped over, spilling the contents onto the floor. On top of everything else, I knew the cross-dressing germaphobe would have serious issues knowing his stuff had been in contact with hotel-grade carpet. But now that the contents had been spilled onto the floor, there was no way to pack it back the way it had been packed. Which meant, I might as well take advantage of the opportunity to see if there was anything in there I could use.

I slid off the bedspread and eased myself onto the floor next to a pile of Ziploc baggies. I piled them back inside the suitcase and found an envelope protruding from an interior pocket. I slipped the envelope out and read the name that had been calligraphied across the heavy weight paper: *Ms. Elli Lisbon.*

My cross-dressing germaphobe was a woman.

Temporarily distracted from far bigger problems, I rooted through the clothes on the floor. Under the red bandana printed maxi-skirt was a white tee with a tiny pocket. Under that was a red canvas bucket hat, red canvas ballerina flats three sizes bigger than my own foot size, and a red and white striped canvas purse. Other outfits were similarly packed: a blue and brown sleeveless sundress with chambray flip flops and an oversized crushable straw hat.

I slid the card from the envelope and read the invitation. *Kick up your heels at the Annual Cattle Baron's Ball!* Said the headline, printed in deep red ink on thick stationery. I glanced back at the bucket hat and the chambray flip flops. Maybe ball meant something different in Texas.

But then, it struck me that Ms. Elli Lisbon and her assortment of weird western clothes might get me out of there safely.

I struggled to my feet, then pushed the western wear aside and traded the poppy printed dress for the prairie skirt. It hung to the floor, perfect for hiding my injured knee and battered white Keds. I pulled on her blue Dodgers T-shirt, then picked up the blue Carmel sweatshirt I'd bought hours earlier and tore it along a seam until I had a square of fabric to tie over my short hair, babushka style. I wasn't concerned with looking stylish or retro or fashionable. My only concern was with not looking like me.

I moved to the hallway and pulled the bathroom door closed to see my reflection. If success could be measured by impromptu Halloween-like attire, it had been achieved. And if I was wrong, I had a good start on an insanity case.

The phone rang. I picked up the extension in the bathroom. Necessity in the form of knee pain forced me to close the toilet and sit on the lid. This was not my proudest moment.

"Hello?"

"Ms. Night? This is Jack Jordan."

"Mr. Jordan—" I started.

"Call me Jack."

"Jack, I'm sorry I had to cancel our meeting tonight. Something came up—I mean, something happened. Something that concerns the hotel."

"Ms. Night—" he started.

"Call me Madison," I said.

"Madison, were you in the hotel bar earlier this evening?"

"Yes, but I had to leave. There are men who followed me here from Dallas. I don't know what they want from me."

"How do you know they followed you?"

"I overheard them. They knew I came in from Dallas. They knew I started my trip on the east coast. One of your hotel members is involved with them. I didn't realize it at first. I was shopping, and when I left the store one of these men was outside waiting for me. I think he was going to force me to go with him, but your hotel concierge appeared and helped me. He walked me back to the hotel and I thought I was safe, until I saw him talking to the men at the bar, so I think he's involved too."

The other end of the phone was silent, and I wondered if Jack Jordan of hotel security was still on the line. "Hello?"

"I'm here, Ms. Ni—Madison. Is that all you want to tell me?"

I wanted to pretend I'd told him everything, but deep down, I knew there was more. "There's another man here, too. Brad Turlington. He and I had a relationship that ended abruptly. I don't know how he knew I was coming here, but he found out and followed me. Mr. Jord—Jack, I do not want to see that man."

"The best way for you to not see that man is to remain in your room, at least for the rest of the night. Can you do that?"

"Yes."

"I'm going to see what I can find out. In the meantime, is there anything I can arrange for you? Have you had dinner?"

"I'm not hungry."

"The kitchen stays open for room service until eleven, so you have a little time if you change your mind."

"Thank you."

After I hung up the phone, I changed out of the makeshift undercover outfit and took another shower, then pulled on a fresh pair of panties and a nightshirt I'd bought at the drug store and crawled into bed. Twenty minutes later I called room service and ordered a Cobb Salad.

I pulled on a pair of white linen pants from Elli's suitcase and refolded the clothes that had fallen onto the floor. The hotel was eerily silent, except for footsteps over my head. The men who occupied that room, who I'd heard talking on the balcony, were moving about. I crossed the carpet and unlocked the balcony doors a crack and listened. Any conversation I might have heard was drowned by the sound of the water crashing on the rocks of Monterey.

I unscrewed the cap from a bottle of sparkling water from the mini fridge. I poured half of it into a plastic cup from the bathroom, settling into the plush armchair next to the sliding glass doors. There was a knock on the door to my room.

"Ms. Night? It's Jack Jordan. I have your room service," said a deep voice.

I set the water on the table and crossed the room to the door. "Just a minute." I hadn't expected the head of security to deliver my food, but, in light of the circumstances, I didn't mind the extra attention. As I reached for the chain that locked the door, I peeked through the peephole and froze.

Jack Jordan, head of security wasn't standing in front of my door.

Harrison the Concierge was. And there was no tray of room service in sight.

SIX

I'D UNDONE THE CHAIN, AND NOW MY FINGERS FUMBLED with it, trying to get it back into place. There was no point in pretending I wasn't in the room. I backed away, stumbling when I connected with the corner of the mattress. With my hands on the surface of the muted turquoise and yellow floral coverlet, I guided myself around the bed to the phone and dialed the operator.

"Yes, Ms. Night?" she answered. For a split second I was spooked by the fact that she knew who was calling.

"Can you please page Jack Jordan again?" I asked in a low whisper.

"Didn't he call you earlier?"

"Yes, but I need to speak to him again."

"Ms. Night, are you okay?"

"There's a man at my door. He's trying to get to me. I'm trapped inside and I need help," I hissed.

"Ms. Night—"

"Hurry!" I said.

I hung up the phone and turned around. There was a click by the door, the slip of a key sliding into the slot. He was coming in after me. I moved past the second of the beds to the curtains by the balcony, my hands searching for the opening. My room was on the third floor, too high for me to jump. The front door opened. I slid the balcony door open further. Harrison entered the room. His eyes went wide as he saw me move through the narrow opening.

"Madison!" he cried out.

I stumbled backward, over the chair I'd rested in earlier, contorted my body and lunged toward the metal railing. Strong arms closed around me from behind, pinning my own arms along the sides of my body. I pushed my head back hard, clunking my skull against his forehead.

"Ow!" he said. He dropped his arms from around my chest to around my waist and picked me up, then carried me back into the room. With his foot he pushed the balcony doors shut, still holding me. I planted my feet on the side of the bed and pushed backward, but with the doors shut, I only succeeded in pushing him up against the glass.

"Shhhhh. Madison, Ms. Night. Calm down. I'm Jack Jordan. Shhh. I'm hotel security. Shhh, shhh. Let me explain."

I had little energy left, little enough that I needed time to rest if I intended to escape. I went limp. He put his hands on my upper arms and turned me around, then lowered me onto the bed. I looked up at him. He reached behind him to the arm chair and pulled it forward, then sat down directly across from me. Before he spoke, he pulled out his wallet and opened it to a pair of identification cards that showed out from under plastic windows. He held the wallet toward me and I took it.

The first card was a driver's license for Jack Jordan. The address was in Carmel By-The-Sea, California. The other card was hotel identification. Again I read his name, next to the title of Hotel Security Manager. Both pictures were of the same man, the man with salt and pepper hair who in front of me. I handed the wallet back.

"I don't understand," I said.

"Your message to me—you were right. There's something going on at the hotel and I'm investigating it. I needed a way to keep tabs on them, so I've been standing in as the hotel concierge. People trust the concierge. People don't trust hotel security."

"So when I checked in, you were undercover?"

"In a manner of speaking. The real concierge has been around at all times, ready to step in and help if need be."

"And outside of the souvenir store, earlier today? How did you happen to be there when I needed you?"

"I've been trying to understand their operation. When you said you had the wrong suitcase, I suspected you might be working with them. I followed you to see where you'd go, what you'd do. Your reaction to Louis made it clear you didn't know him."

"I can't shake the feeling he wanted something from me, I just don't know what."

"You're a noticeable woman, Madison, with your fluffy blond hair and aqua outfit. Even in a town filled with tourists, it's not that strange Louis remembered you from your meeting by the elevator. Add in the crutches, and, well, let's just say you're not going to fly under the radar. He probably picked you out of the crowd just like I did. If you look like you look, especially in a town with Doris Day history, you're going to get noticed. It's likely he just wanted to talk to a pretty lady."

"And you—you were the concierge. The letter you sent to my room was signed Jack Jordan. That's why I asked to meet you for a drink."

"The letter was for real. You suspected we had a foul-up. I had to make sure we didn't, otherwise it would raise questions about how we were running the hotel. Turns out the foul up was in Dallas."

"Dallas…" I said slowly. "That's why I thought the men were after me. I heard them say 'she's coming in from Dallas.' I thought they meant me." I paused. "Who did they mean?"

"Are you traveling with something valuable?" he asked.

"Right now I'm traveling with little more than the clothes I'm wearing and they aren't even mine."

"But in your real suitcase, was there something with a high value?"

I thought for a moment about the double-knit polyester outfits I'd packed, the four tubes of sunscreen, the assortment of Keds, and the collapsible straw hat to keep me shielded from the sun. I seriously doubted the whole lot would be worth over a couple hundred dollars, tops. Before I could answer, Jack continued.

"I have reason to believe they're expecting a package

that was routed through Dallas, something that might've been on your flight. There's a good chance their package never arrived or went to someone else, just like your suitcase did."

"But they knew I stopped in Dallas on my way from the east coast."

Jack scratched his head, his salt-and-pepper hair mussed up. "Madison, I don't think the east coast they mentioned is the one you came from."

"I don't understand."

"Those men weren't talking about you. They're talking about the east Barbary Coast."

"Africa?"

He nodded. "You said they called it 'she'?"

"Yes, that's why I thought they meant me."

"Madison, they're not here to pick up you. I think they're here to pick up an extremely rare, rough cut diamond."

SEVEN

"AND WHAT ABOUT THE OTHER MAN? HOW IS HE INVOLVED?"
I asked tentatively.

"That's where I'm stumped. I ran the name you gave me, 'Brad Turlington,' through the hotel reservations and there's no record of him."

"You were talking to him at the bar while I was waiting. It was you, and him and two other guys. You were arguing."

"I was at the bar, yes. A couple of guys were talking baseball. Things got heated. Those two guys know me as the concierge. As long as I'm here, I have to treat every person who I see like a guest, for the sake of the hotel. Are you sure you didn't make a mistake?"

I had been sure. As sure as I'd been the man sitting in front of me was involved in something crooked, as sure as I'd been the men above me were out to kidnap me. I'd been as sure as when I'd thought I had the suitcase of a cross-dresser from Dallas, and as sure as I'd been months ago when I thought I had everything I'd ever needed out of life.

I wanted to believe I hadn't seen Brad. I wanted to believe I'd left him behind when I left Pennsylvania, that I'd moved on.

"Madison, look at me."

I looked up from my hands to the face of the security manager. The sun had etched lines of maturity into his face, but his ruddy complexion lent him a youthful appearance.

"Madison, why did you react the way you did? When I came into your room. Like you were fighting for your life?"

"Because I am," I said. I stared behind him at the bright white baseboard that joined the textured wheat wallpaper to the muted tones of the carpet. A soft ivory, or better yet, a taupe would have been better complement to the décor.

I shut my eyes, blocking out the decorator's instinct to improve the room and thought about my actions. When I opened my eyes, I looked Jack in the eyes.

"This trip was meant as a way for me to get away from what's going on in my life right now." Or not going on, as the case may be. "I need a fresh start, but before I can look forward I have to shake this feeling that another shoe is about to drop."

"You had a bad scare. Anybody would have reacted the way you did. I'm going to keep looking out for you because that's my job, but I have to tell you I don't know anything about this third man. As far as I can tell, there's only the two of them, and nobody followed you here, from Dallas or from Pennsylvania. Can you believe that?"

"I guess I have to."

"I think you should stay in for the rest of the night," he said.

"I will. Wait, where's my dinner?"

"What dinner?"

"I called for room service. You even said you had it. Before I opened the door."

"I did, didn't I?" he turned around and looked at the door, then scratched his head. "After we talked, I asked the front desk and the operator to let me know if you made or received any calls. They told me you called in a dinner order. I figured you might freak out when you saw who I was, so I used that to get you to the door."

"So where's my food?"

"They didn't have an order. I figured you changed your mind." He looked at the clock behind him. "But it's late, the kitchen's closed now. I don't know what happened to your food, but how about I get you something from town? You like pizza?"

"You don't have to do that," I said, only half-meaning it.

"Then let the hotel pick up your breakfast tomorrow morning. Give your name to the restaurant hostess and she'll take care of the bill."

"Thank you, Jack."

"Are you going to be okay by yourself?"

"You don't happen to keep spare pets around the hotel, do you?" I asked.

"You know, it's not a bad idea. Maybe I should suggest it to Ms. Day." He smiled warmly.

I stood and walked him to the door.

"Good night, Madison. Try to get some sleep. I'll check on you tomorrow."

He opened the door to my room and stepped into the hallway, nearly tripping over a room service tray on the carpet in front of the door.

"What the—?"

"I didn't hear a knock. Did you hear a knock?" I asked.

His face clouded. "No, I didn't hear a knock." He bent down and picked up the tray, then carried it past me into the room. "Where do you want it?"

"Bed's fine."

He set the tray on the bed. A silver dome covered a plate that sat on the center of a white doily-like mat. Tucked under the plate was a white envelope. Jack picked up the envelope, tapped it twice on the edge of the tray, and held it up. "Dinner's on me."

"I ordered a lot of food. You might want to look at the bill before you make that kind of offer."

He raised an eyebrow then made a showing of peeking into the envelope. Within moments the humor left his face, replaced with a creased forehead and a downturned mouth.

"I was kidding. I ordered a Cobb Salad. How much could that be?" I asked, straining forward to see the bill.

He looked up and stared at me for an uncomfortable amount of time.

"Jack? What is it?"

"Nothing." He slid the envelope into the back pocket of his pants. "Stay put tonight, Madison. And make sure you lock the door."

An uneasiness swept over me, like the chill that shudders through your body seconds after biting into ice. I started to shut the door and the phone rang. Before the latch connected on the door, Jack pushed back inside.

"Does anybody know your room number?" he asked.

"I don't think so."

"Then pick up the receiver. but don't say anything."

The shrill ringing continued in the background. "Won't it be better to let it ring?"

"No."

On his instructions, I picked up the receiver and held it to my head. The line crackled. Jack stood next to me, and I angled the device so it pointed to the ceiling, so we both had a chance at hearing. He held a finger up to his mouth to remind me to be quiet.

"That wasn't very bright, skipping out on us tonight," said a male voice. "Don't try to hide. We're watching you." The line cracked a bit more, and then there was a click.

"They know I was at the bar, that I saw them and left. I don't like this," I said.

"I don't think that message was for you." Jack dialed zero on the phone and spoke into the receiver. "Hi Sophie, this is Mr. Jordan. A call came in to 319 just now. What can you tell me about it?"

I heard a tinny voice through the receiver, picking out only the occasional word. "Ms. Night wants privacy for the rest of the night. If anybody rings her room, either get a message or forward it to my room. Is that clear?"

He hung up the receiver. "Madison, I don't know what to tell you. Our operator asked someone to cover the booth while she stepped out for a break. She doesn't know anything about the call—if it came from inside the hotel our outside. I know you're worried, but you won't be interrupted again. Can I do anything else to make you more comfortable?"

"I don't suppose you'd be willing to share a room with me tonight, would you?" I said, not quite believing the words coming out of my mouth. Too many unexpected things had happened since I'd arrived in Carmel, and I didn't want to be alone. "There are two beds, after all." I felt my face go hot. "I'm sorry, I shouldn't have asked. I don't know what came over me," I added.

He blushed. "It's okay. Under the circumstances, I'm surprised it took so long for you to ask. And even though I can appreciate the request, I have to decline. There's someone at home waiting for me."

This time the blush crept over my face, and didn't leave until well after I locked the door behind him.

After Jack left, I wandered to the room service tray and looked under the silver dome. My appetite was no longer an issue. I put the dome back on top of the plate and moved it back into the hall, then hung the Do Not Disturb sign on the door and put the chain in place. I changed out of the maxi skirt and crawled into the bed in my underwear.

I AWOKE in the middle of the night. The room was a cocoon of darkness and the only sound was that of pacing over my head. Someone above me was very much awake. The clock read three-thirty. There were too many hours between now and dawn for me to consider anything other than staying put safely under the covers.

I thought about what Jack had said earlier. He checked out the people I thought I'd seen, and Brad hadn't been one of them. Was it possible I was so desperate to believe he'd follow me that I was seeing him in places where he wasn't? And if so, how long until the memory of him faded and I could go on with my life, life as Madison Night, single forty-something? I'd heard statistics about single women in their forties, statistics more in favor of lightning striking than finding a relationship. I didn't want a relationship anymore. I'd figure out a way to get everything I wanted out of life and I'd do it all for me. Who knows? When I figured out where I wanted to live, maybe I'd even get a dog.

The footsteps over my head continued in a random cycle. I pictured someone crossing the room, stopping to look out the window, then crossing back. That's it, I realized. Whatever it is they're looking for out their window, maybe I'll see it, too. I pushed the covers back and eased myself onto the floor, then quietly hobbled to the curtains and the magnificent view I'd been ignoring.

Earlier, before I'd considered that there was a threat to my presence, I'd stood on the balcony and stared at the view. The dark blue water had crashed against the rocky Monterey cliffs in the distance while the sun cast shimmering highlights over the beach, the sand, the horizon, and the ocean. But now, in the middle of the night, I saw none of that. What I saw was a flickering light, flashing at equally repeated intervals, from the sidewalk half a block from the hotel. Flash-Flash-Flash. Pause. Flash Flash Flash. Pause. I strained my eyes to make out the figure with the light, but I couldn't. Aside from the light, there was nothing decipherable about the scene.

The phone jangled a tortured ring. I jumped. My heart pounded in my chest and adrenaline shot through my arms and legs. I stared at the machine on the table between the beds. Jack had given instructions not to allow any calls into my room. Was this a call for me that had been screened?

I gripped the long curtains and stared at the phone, wishing for a sign. After twelve rings, the phone stopped. I crawled across the bed, closer to the windows, and sat next to the phone, waiting. When it started ringing a second time, I was equally scared. I picked up the receiver after one ring and held it to my head, not saying a word.

"You saw the signal. Now it's time for us to see the pretty lady," said a low voice. "You have fifteen minutes." The line disconnected.

I didn't know how to reach Jack. I sat on the bed, considering my options for about forty-five seconds. When nothing else came to mind, I dialed the operator.

"Good evening, Ms. Night," said a female voice.

"Hi, is there a way to get a message to Mr. Jordan?" I asked in a hushed voice. I kept one hand cupped around the receiver so my voice wouldn't carry.

"Ms. Night? I think there's a problem with our connection. I can barely hear you," said the woman.

I cleared my throat. "Mr. Jordan left instructions for you to keep calls from coming through to my room, but one just did. I need to talk to him to tell him what the caller said. I know it's late, but is there a way to reach him? An emergency number?"

"Ms. Night, Mr. Jordan gave me no such instruction."

"Yes, he did. I was sitting right next to him when he told you."

"I'm sorry, Ms. Night, but I don't know what you're talking about. Jack Jordan left no such instruction. In fact, I haven't spoken to Mr. Jordan since he returned from his vacation last week."

EIGHT

"Is this Sophie?"

"Sophie who?"

"Sophie the operator. Mr. Jordan called the operator 'Sophie' earlier."

"Ms. Night, we don't have an operator named Sophie. Are you okay?"

"No, I'm not. I'm coming to the lobby."

"Ms. Night—" the operator started, but I set the receiver back into the cradle before letting her finish her thought.

It was a few minutes after four. The sun wouldn't be up for another hour or so, but I wasn't comfortable staying in my room. Something was happening, something that had to do with me, and I wasn't going to stick around to let it happen. I knew my injured knee would hinder any chance of leaving the hotel, but the idea of staying was worse than that of trying to get away.

I wrapped my knee, redressed in the maxi skirt, and pulled the Dodgers T-shirt over my head. I slicked my hair back with hotel moisturizer, stepped back into my sneakers, grabbed my crutches, and locked the door behind me.

The hallways were empty. I winced every time the crutches made a sound, but made it to the elevators and traveled down to the ground level. It took longer than I'd thought to move to the lobby of the hotel. I hid behind a column and leaned forward, looking at the concierge desk. The first place I'd seen Jack Jordan had been at that concierge desk and I hoped, desperately, he wasn't there again. A woman in a white shirt, thin black necktie, and black blazer stood behind the desk tapping keys on the hidden keyboard. Her hair was parted on the side and slicked back into a tight bun she wore at the nape of her neck. Her nametag said Kitty. Other than a thick coat of scarlet red color on her lips, her face appeared un-made-up.

Slowly, I approached her.

She looked up and smiled.

"Good morning," she said in a cheerful voice. "Or at least it will be morning soon, I guess."

"Good morning. Can you tell me what time the sun comes up?"

"Yes, I can," she said with a smile. She waited a beat for me to acknowledge that technically she'd answered my question, but I wasn't in the mood for jokes.

"What time?" I prompted.

She leaned forward over the surface of the concierge

desk and looked at the door, then pulled herself back and looked at her watch. "You'll see a glow in about ten minutes. Everything turns kind of an orangey gold. You'll see the sun shortly after that, maybe fifteen, maybe twenty minutes. In forty-five it'll will be hard for our guests to sleep if they didn't shut their curtains."

"Thank you," I said, starting toward the door.

"It's still pretty dark out. Would you like a flashlight?"

I turned back to her, poised atop the crutches. "I don't know if I can maneuver these and hold a flashlight, too."

"Where are you going?"

"I'm an early bird. I thought I'd go to the beach, sit on one of the rocks by the road, and listen to the waves."

"I broke my leg last year and was on crutches for a solid three months. It's a bitch getting down the slope of Ocean Avenue with them. Hold on."

She disappeared behind a door to the left of her. I tapped my fingers on the marble counter, eager for her to return. I didn't know what kind of time I had but I didn't think I had much.

From farther inside the hotel I heard a soft ding. The elevator. I quickly grabbed the crutches and moved to a yellow gingham sofa. I propped the crutches behind another column, out of sight. I reclined, pulling the fabric of the maxi skirt around my legs. I rolled into the back of the sofa and hoped I looked like someone who had chosen not to sleep in their room.

"Where is she?" asked a familiar voice. It was same man who had cornered me in front of the drug store before Jack Jordan had come to my rescue, before Jack

Jordan turned out to be not who he'd seemed. It was Louis.

"She was here a second ago," said Kitty.

I curled back into a ball on the sofa but kept my head raised so I could hear their conversation.

"Did you see which way she went?"

An awkward silence followed. My mind pictured a thousand permutations of what was going on. I imagined the man seeing the crutches I'd stashed behind the column and coming over to me, to do—to do what I didn't know, only, I was convinced it wasn't going to be good.

"She said she was going to the ocean."

"At this hour?" Louis asked. "Sounds suspicious."

"That's what I thought. I said I was getting her a flashlight, but she must have left without it."

"Tell you what, Kitty, I'll look for her. The ocean, you said?"

"That's what she said."

I waited on the sofa, considering my options. I could go back to my room, or I could follow Louis, the man from the elevators. After the front door to the hotel shut, I stood and flexed my legs individually, then spied a small flat rectangle on the lobby floor. A room key tucked into a paper sleeve. I felt my pockets for my own key. It was where I'd tucked it, in the pocket of the skirt.

I bent down to pick up the keycard when Kitty called out to me. "There you are!"

"I had to go back to my room for something, but I must have dropped my key." I flipped the sleeve over. The number 419 was written on the back. I looked at the front doors, then quickly looked back down at the keycard. Louis had dropped this.

"Looks like the sun is starting to come up. I won't need that flashlight after all." A cloudy plan formed in my mind. I made a show of fussing with my crutches and hobbling out the front door, then tossed them by the flower beds that decorated the walk-up entrance to the hotel. Adrenaline coursed through my body and eliminated any pain that had been there days earlier. In the dark, I moved to the side of the hotel and reentered through another door.

I picked up the receiver on the hotel phone that sat next to the ugly lamp on the marble table across from the elevators. I dialed 419. I counted at least ten rings, a good indication that the room was empty. With one hand on the wall, I moved through the hallway to the elevator, then hit the button for the third floor. A plan had formed, but first I needed to better my disguise.

In my room, I emptied a packet of instant coffee into a hotel glass and added enough of the serum from Elli Lisbon's overnight kit to make a paste with my fingers. I raked the resulting brown glop through my hair, temporarily turning myself from a blonde to a brunette. Next, I swept my face generously with bronzer, then changed from the bandana printed skirt into a pair of white linen drawstring-waist pants, the faded Dodgers T-shirt, and a dark brown cowboy hat. I looked at myself one last time and was shocked by the stranger in the mirror.

I dialed 419 and heard the ringing phone through the ceiling. Five rings, then six, then seven. When I hit double digits, I knew no one would answer. I left the room and returned to the elevator, riding up one floor. I followed the same path I'd been following to get to my room one floor below, took three quick breaths to pump up my courage, and shoved the keycard into the door. I held my own key in the opposite hand, prepared with a cover story if anyone were to discover me. Nobody did.

The light outside the door turned to a bright lime green. Quietly, I turned the brushed chrome handle and pushed the door inside, then closed the door behind me. I waited for a couple of seconds to make sure I was indeed alone, then moved further inside and turned on the light.

Both beds were made. There were no signs of luggage or personal belongings. I fed my hand between the thick fabric of the curtains and held it open far enough to make out a few figures on the street by the waterfront. Where earlier I'd seen the flashing light, now I saw the outline of two men, one holding the other at gunpoint. Even from a distance I could tell the man with his hands in the air was Jack Jordan.

NINE

The scene was far worse than I'd expected. I needed to call someone—maybe the front desk, maybe 911—and tell them a man was about to be shot by the waterfront, when both men turned and faced the hotel. The man with the gun was Louis.

As I stood there, as still as I could, I realized that I'd made the biggest mistake of my life by turning on the lights. If they'd been able to signal to each other earlier, then surely, they'd be able to see me, now.

Jack Jordan clasped his hands together and brought them down on the back of the other man's head. Louis fell to the ground and dropped the gun. Jack picked it up and jogged up the hill.

I knew I couldn't go back to my room. That would be the first place Jack would look for me. I started to leave, tripping over the corner of the bedspread. I heard a sound by the door, mechanisms inside the keycard lock that had tumbled. I was trapped.

I scanned the room for a hiding place. If I got past the beds and found the opening between the curtains I could open the sliding door to the balcony and hide outside, but for how long? The idea of falling down four stories was about as appealing as being caught in the room red-handed.

My right hand was on the closet door, which slid open an inch. As the door to the room opened up, I squeezed into the closet and slid the door shut behind me. I waited, with my heart pounding in my chest, for someone to open the doors and expose me.

I pressed myself backward, despite the pressure of something already in the closet digging into my thigh. A safe, probably, or luggage stand. I knew the importance of remaining still despite the discomfort. I only wished the occupants of room 419 had taken the time to hang up their clothes so I'd have something to hide behind.

"I'm telling you, the light came from this room. I've been watching the windows all night. I didn't make a mistake," said a male voice.

I froze. It was Jack.

"I don't know what kind of game you're playing, but there's nobody here," said another voice. It was the other man from the elevators that first day. That meant Louis was most likely the person who'd been knocked out by the waterfront.

"Check the balcony," commanded Jack. "I'll check the closet."

I felt the hand connect with the door to the closet before it slid to the side, leaving me face to face with Jack Jordan.

His eyes went wide for a second. He held a finger up to his mouth to silence me, then mouthed the words. "Trust me." He slid the door shut as quickly as he'd opened it, leaving me speechless.

"You're wasting my time, Jordan. Where is she? I've traveled a long way and spent a lot of money and I'm not leaving without her."

"I'm telling you, something's not right. We have to get out of this hotel."

"No. This time I'm telling you what we're going to do. You're going to give me the lady and I'm going to walk out of here and head back to Los Angeles. She's going to be on a plane by midnight and I'm going to be a millionaire."

"That's not what we agreed on."

"Yeah? Well, things changed when you knocked out Louis. He's been keeping an eye on the lady since she got here and now he's out of the picture thanks to you. Makes me wonder if you've been planning a double cross all along."

"Louis is the one who pulled the double cross. I was just taking care of myself," said Jack.

"Not sure I believe you."

There was silence, and I pictured the two men facing off, each with a pistol aimed at each other, waiting to see who was going to shoot first.

"Get the lady," commanded the unnamed man.

"First, I want to see the money," said Jack.

"The money's in the safe in the closet. You'll get it when I see her."

Before I could figure out how exactly I was going to master the art of transmogrifying, there was a knock on the door. I held my breath and listened for something, anything.

"See who that is," said Jack.

Soft footsteps, muffled in carpet, walked past me to the door.

"It's the cops," said the other man.

Another set of footsteps crossed the room, then, a dull thud. Someone grunted, then something large fell to the floor.

I couldn't see how any of that was good.

The closet door slid open. Jack Jordan grabbed my wrist and pulled me out. Gray suit's body lay slumped on the floor.

"There's a man in a uniform outside this door. He is not a cop. He is not going to expect to see you. Use that element of surprise and get out of here. Go to your room—no." His eyes darted to my face and past me to the door. "Go to the lobby. There's a diner across the street. It won't be empty. Go there, get a booth, and wait for me. Don't talk to anybody, don't tell anybody what's happened."

"You're crazy!" I hissed. I pulled away from him, but his grip on my wrists tightened.

"There's no time for me to explain what's going on. You have to trust me."

"No," I said in a barely audible whisper. "The cops are here to help me."

The pounding on the door resumed. Jack stepped away from me and peered through the peephole, then came back. He put his hands on my forearms and squared me off. "When you open the door, look at the officer. Decide for yourself if you should trust him or not."

"Why should I listen to you?" I asked.

Unexpectedly, he put his arms around me and hugged me, pinning my arms to my sides. "I know I'm asking a lot of a stranger," he whispered in my left ear. He released his hug and stepped back, waiting to see what I would do next. "If you believe he's a real cop, then tell him everything." He let go of me.

I stepped away from Jack, my back pressed against the wall. I searched his face for something reassuring but saw nothing. I stepped past him. When I reached the door, I looked to Jack one last time. He wasn't there. I tucked my chin and braced myself. I pulled the door open.

I recognized the uniformed officer who stood in the hallway. He had longish blond hair tucked behind his ears and a mole under his left eye. He was the man who had driven me from the airport to the hotel. He was not a cop.

Jack was telling the truth.

I sucked in a deep breath of air and pushed past him as instructed, then ran as fast as I could into the hallway, down the hall, to the elevator. My knee pulsed, but adrenaline kept me moving. I jabbed the up and down buttons by the elevator. The up button lit up first and I hopped inside and pressed Door Close. My heart pounded in my chest like a chef pounding out a chicken breast with a wooden mallet. I didn't care I was going up without an escape route. Up was better than where I had been, and after going up my only problem would be getting back down. I could deal with problems like that.

And then elevator stopped on the eleventh floor. The doors eased open and a fresh new problem confronted me.

I was face to face with Brad.

TEN

I slapped at the panel of buttons on the wall. One of the buttons screamed the alarm. The doors slid shut. Brad didn't move. I gulped deep breaths and punched the lobby button repeatedly, as if it would make the elevator travel faster. I looked around the elevator for a hidden security camera, something that indicated that there was a chance I wasn't really all alone. Aside from the reflection of the brunette stranger in a cowboy hat and Dodgers T-shirt in the mirrored ceiling, I saw nothing.

When I landed in the lobby several older couples stood around in nylon jog suits and bright white sneakers, as if their trip to Carmel had required new workout clothes. A police officer stood by the front door. I didn't know if he was real or not. My knee throbbed but I headed past the early birds to the front door anyway, in search of the crutches I'd abandoned in the front garden beds earlier that morning.

"I don't know who she is," I heard. I looked in the direction of the voice and saw Kitty from the front desk talking to a man in a black suit and tie. "She was here right before Louis left. He found her crutches out front. I don't know where she went."

"Did you see her leave the hotel?" asked the man.

"No."

"Can you describe her?" he asked.

"She looks like, well, she looks like that," She pointed to a poster from *Midnight Lace* that hung on the wall of the hotel. By her feet a small dog wound circles around her leg, circling her with a blue leash.

"She looks like Doris Day?"

"Pretty much. She has fluffy blond hair and a cute freckled nose. She's thin and wore a floral dress. She smiled a lot."

The man studied the poster on the wall for a few more seconds. "Always liked her," he said, as if he were talking to himself.

I stood to the side of the column, weighing my options. On one hand I could approach the man talking to Kitty, tell him what I'd been through, and hope he was somehow able to help me. There had to be a reason he was asking her about me. On the other hand, I didn't know *why* he was asking about me. I caught my reflection in the glass frame of the *Midnight Lace* movie poster and gasped. Brown streaks from the temporary coffee-hair color ran down the side of my face like skinny sideburns and dripped onto the collar of the T-shirt. I looked a wreck.

And suddenly I knew Brad hadn't recognized me.

I inhaled deeply and blew the air out of my mouth. I straightened my posture and walked out of the hotel as though I was balancing a book on the top of my head: confident, smooth, injury-free. The doctors had told me I would know when I was well enough to start walking without the crutches, and right now, I knew. Even though pain shot through my leg at evenly spaced intervals, I faked good health until I reached the sidewalk, then crossed the street and entered the diner Jack had mentioned.

A rotund man in a stained apron approached my table. I ordered a cup of coffee and a Denver omelet before realizing I had no money to pay. I unzipped the small red and white cotton purse I'd slung across my body, hoping Elli had left behind enough emergency cash to buy me breakfast in a somewhat overpriced diner in Carmel By-The-Sea. I didn't come up with any cash, but I came up with a small black velvet pouch.

With my right hand shaking, I felt the bulging contents through the velvet. As if the shaking was contagious, my left hand shook as I undid the knot in the drawstring. I fed two fingers into the small opening and spread the fabric apart, then looked inside at the base of a small light bulb.

Not what I'd expected.

The waiter returned and filled the chipped beige coffee mug on the table with steaming hot coffee. I dropped the pouch into my lap and covered it with my napkin. I couldn't tell if he'd seen it or not, but until I knew what it meant I didn't want anybody else to know I had it. I leaned in and busied myself with pulling the top off a small plastic cup of creamer, then dumped it into my mug and stirred. I kept up the routine until the waiter was back behind the counter, then tapped the spoon on the side of the mug and set it into onto the table.

What did it mean? I wondered. Had this pouch been filled with a diamond at one point like Jack had told me? And if so, where was it now? Had it ever been in the pouch? Or had this been a double-cross all along?

I drank from the chipped coffee mug and considered other questions. Where had the pouch come from? Even if I didn't agree with her choice of baseball teams, it seemed unlikely that Elli, the very stranger whose luggage I'd ended up with, was really a jewel thief and a double-crossing smuggler. But how else could I have come to be in possession of this pouch?

I closed my eyes for a second and thought back over what had happened earlier. I'd hidden in the room, in the closet. Jack had been the one who exposed me hiding in the closet. He asked me to trust him and he arranged a way for me to get out of there. And then he hugged me.

He must have planted the pouch on me during the hug.

I'd been oblivious to everything at that moment—everything except getting away.

It clicked into place. He was the one who'd told me to stay in my room. He was the one who knew my story, who pretended to protect me by asking the operator to screen my calls. It had been his idea for me to disguise myself, so no one else would recognize me. If he'd hidden the pouch on me, nobody else would think I was connected to him when he came to collect.

And one last thought hit me. It had been his idea for me to go to the diner.

A collection of bells announced new customers. I looked up at the door and clutched the black velvet pouch tightly in my left hand. Jack headed directly toward my table, followed by the man in the black suit from the lobby.

ELEVEN

They slid into the booth across from me. I felt like a scared rabbit must feel when hunting dogs close in. A small, vulnerable animal with no avenue for escape.

"You did good back there," said Jack.

"Who are you people?"

"We have to leave, Ms. Night," said the man in the suit.

"I'm not leaving with either one of you until I know who you are and what this is about."

The two men looked at each other, then the man in the suit nodded at Jack.

"Madison, I want you to meet my partner," Jack said. "This is Special Agent Hamilton Reed."

"Ms. Night, you are in possession of something illegal. You need to come with us."

"The only thing I'm in possession of is a light bulb. You want it? It's yours." I fished my fingers into the black velvet pouch, then set the small bulb on the table next to the salt shaker.

"Keep your voice down, Madison," Jack said.

The two men looked at each other. Jack stifled a smile. Agent Reed stood up. I looked back and forth between their faces. Agent Reed sat back down. Jack put his forearms on the table and leaned in.

"What are you afraid of, Mr. Jordan?" I asked in as casual of a voice that I could muster. I used his last name on purpose. I didn't want to feel like we were on comfortable terms anymore. I wanted to go back to the strained formality we'd had yesterday. I reached out and palmed the light bulb and put it back into the pouch. "Surely you don't think I had anything to do with—with—with the disappearance of the lady," I finished.

Agent Reed's eyes widened. "The lady?"

"Yes. The lady who came from Dallas. Mr. Jordan knows who I mean. Don't you?"

Jack turned to the special agent. "Get us some coffee. I need to talk to her alone."

Agent Reed slid from the booth and took up a position at the counter. He briefly spoke to the cook, then raised a knee and half-sat on a worn green vinyl swivel stool with rust peeking from the joints. They weren't half bad, those stools. Sand the rust, redip them in chrome, reupholster the vinyl—

"Give me the pouch."

"Sure," I said. "I can't see why anybody would want it anyway."

I set the pouch on the table in front of his arms. He kept

his arms crossed for a few seconds while he considered it. "When did you realize it was a light bulb?"

"When I looked inside. I wanted to know what this is about," I demanded. I expected him to refuse or to clam up.

"Why?" he asked, catching me off guard.

"Why what?" I repeated.

"Why do you care? It has nothing to do with you."

"You lied to me. When I told you about Brad Turlington, you said he was a figment of my imagination. That's not true. When I ran past the cop outside of 419, I came face to face with him. It's him. I know it's him. *I know it's him.*"

Jack leaned forward. "Describe this guy to me."

I closed my eyes for a second, breathing in the memory of Brad. "Tall, thin. Curly black hair. Sideburns. Glasses. He has on an orange plaid shirt and khaki trousers. Purple converse sneakers. He's wearing a gold watch, a vintage Rolex, and he smells like Old Spice. He must have gotten caught in the sun yesterday because the tip of his nose is sunburned." I was surprised by the level of detail I recalled of Brad from the split second I'd seen him in front of the elevator.

"What did he do when he saw you?" he asked.

I opened my eyes and stared at the chipped coffee mug. "Nothing. He didn't recognize me," I said quietly.

Tears filled my eyes, tears I tried to blink back. Instead, they overflowed and ran in streaks down my cheeks, dripping bronzer-colored drops onto the white napkin in my lap. I swiped at the tears and inhaled sharply through my nose.

"Wait here." Jack slid from the booth and joined Agent Reed. I willed myself to get control of my emotions.

I hadn't wanted to believe it was over, but after I'd left the hospital, I wanted nothing more than to move on. In time I'd stop looking for him around every corner. With time I'd learn to shut myself off so this would never happen again. I had come to Carmel to get away, to make a break, to clear my mind. I'd been emotionally vulnerable when I'd landed at the airport and I'd let that vulnerability turn into a paranoid roller coaster ride. Enough. I would not let Brad continue to erode my emotional stability.

I looked out the window of the diner toward the hotel. Men in painter's caps and overalls carried supplies through the front door. A white van was parallel-parked in front of the lawn. On the side of the van was a familiar logo: Pierot's Interior Design.

I knew the logo. I knew it all too well. Pierot's was the furniture store where Brad and I had met back in Philadelphia, when it was owned by Mr. Pierot, soon to retire. It was where Brad had taken me under his wing and taught me about Mid-Century Modern design, the store that I ran while he traveled the country taking interior design jobs. It was where I learned how to acquire merchandise for resale without breaking the bank. I narrowed my eyes as I wondered what the van was doing in California, then remembered when he'd ordered the signs—magnets, really—with the Pierot's logo, to add a bit of professionalism to his freelance team when he took jobs around the country.

Jobs around the country. Like Carmel By-The-Sea.

To Doris Day's hotel, currently under renovation before the annual Carmel Art Festival. That's why it had all seemed familiar. Brad had bid on this job when we were still together.

Another man opened the van and put a floor lamp inside. I recognized the style immediately, a product of the fifties atomic era that captured the whimsical impact that technology and outer space had inflicted on interior design. It was my single favorite design aesthetic, the one category where Brad and I disagreed when he trained me to be an interior decorator. He liked the minimalism of the mid-fifties, the planes of Danish modern, the simplicity of George Nelson and Charles Eames. I did too, but I was also drawn to the sillier aspect of midcentury design: yellow walls, sputnik lamps, radial clocks, donut phones, and boomerang tables. Where Brad's sense of decorating was rooted in wood, mine was rooted in laminate. He'd tried to change my tastes, but it hadn't worked. Eventually, he blamed it on my fascination with Doris Day movies, something he knew he could never undo.

And here I was, sitting in a diner across the street from the hotel Doris Day owned in Carmel, watching a man in overalls carry furniture out of the hotel, furniture that by anybody's account had been handpicked to make the place something special.

In a moment, as I sat watching the man in overalls load items from the hotel into the back of the van, it occurred to me that everything I'd seen, everything I'd heard, everything I'd imagined, made sense if I trusted one man's information.

"Jack," I called out suddenly. "I know where to find the diamond."

The two men looked at me. I stared out the window, glued to the scene. I was right. I knew I was right. Now I just needed to make sure the right men believed me.

Special Agent Reed paid for my coffee and we left.

"Follow me," I said, heading back to the hotel.

As I walked, I scanned the crowds of people already pouring onto the streets. Carmel By-The-Sea was a walking town, and by the looks of it, it was a morning town, too. Cars were in the way more than they were a convenience factor. I'd noticed most of the tourists parked their cars when they arrived and didn't move them again until the day they left.

A bicycle cop poised on his bike in the driveway between two hotels. His uniform matched that of the officer who had come to the hotel room earlier.

"Excuse me!" I called out to him before Jack or Agent Reed could respond.

The officer shielded his eyes and looked at me, but didn't respond. I crossed the street and closed the distance between us until I was right in front of him.

I took two deep breaths, one for courage and one because I was out of breath, then started talking. "Hi. I'm Madison Night. I'm staying at that hotel and there's something criminal going on in there. Some kind of jewel heist. Did you see the men who followed me out of the diner?" I asked.

I turned to look behind me and shielded my own eyes. Jack and Special Agent Reed were gone. I turned back to the officer, who was still staring at me. "I don't know where they went. Anyway, this is important. See that van in front of the hotel?" I pointed to the Pierot van. "Those aren't real decorators. They're faking it. They're pretending so they can take something valuable from the hotel."

The officer looked over my shoulder, then back at me. "I'll keep an eye on them."

"You believe me? Do you want to take my name down for a statement or something?"

"That won't be necessary. I'll take it from here."

That's exactly what I wanted to hear. "Thank you, officer," I said, all the while knowing the man I spoke to was faking his own identity as much as I had been faking my information.

I returned to the hotel lobby and found Jack and Agent Reed sitting by the fireplace. I wasn't terribly surprised they'd left me. I eased myself into the seat in front of them. My back was to the concierge desk.

"Here's what's going to happen—" I started.

"Ms. Night, with all due respect, you're not the one calling the shots," said Special Agent Reed.

I crossed my arms and leaned forward. "Do you know what's going on?" I asked Agent Reed. When he didn't answer, I turned to Jack. "Do you?" I waited a couple of seconds.

"Listen to the lady, Reed," said Jack.

Agent Reed crossed his own arms to mirror my body language. I wasn't sure if he was going to say something or not. He didn't.

"The cop I approached out front is not a cop, but he thinks that I think he is. I told him to follow the men unloading the furniture from the hotel because they're not really decorators and they're trying to smuggle something valuable from the hotel."

"Why do you think those men aren't really decorators?" Reed asked.

"They are decorators—that's the point. The fake cop doesn't know that, so now he's off on a wild goose chase."

Neither Reed nor Jack reacted, so I knew the information I'd spoken so far wasn't news. I continued. "The diamond isn't in that van. It's safe. But if you want to make sure the men from 419 don't get her, we have to act fast."

"Ms. Night, thank you for your help, we'll take it from here," said Special Agent Reed. He stood up from the table and turned to Jack. "I'm going after the decorators."

Jack nodded, then turned to me. "What else have you figured out?"

Jack Jordan had been the only person to investigate what I'd said so far. If anybody was going to listen to me, I suspected it would be him.

"The men loading the truck out front are probably freelancers. I didn't think about that when I made the reservation, but Brad's been applying for jobs around the country, trying to build his client base and his reputation. The hotel is under renovation. Brad must have hired local talent when he took the job. He doesn't have a staff in California and it would be cheaper to hire someone here then to pay people to travel with him. You already told me

Brad's not on the guest list. He's here to work, not to play. That's why his name isn't in the system. He's not part of the problem."

"Go on."

"The cop on the bicycle was wearing the same uniform as the man you knocked out upstairs. It says Carmel, NY."

"And you told him to follow the decorators?"

"I figured it was the only way to get him away from the hotel."

"But they're decorators," Jack said.

"Yes. They're probably putting items in temporary storage so they can paint the place."

He held out a hand. I grabbed it and he pulled me up. "Were you telling the truth, Ms. Night? You know where the rock is?"

"Yes."

"Good. I'm going to visit our friends. You get the rock. Meet me as soon as you can."

"You want me to get it?"

"You're the one who's undercover," he said, with a hint of a smile pulling at the corner of this mouth.

"Where do you want me to meet you?"

"I'll let you figure that out, too."

He left before I could tell him I seriously had no idea.

TWELVE

Jack Jordan walked past the front desk while I remained in the hotel lobby. Kitty glanced up at him but didn't seem to recognize him. It was a piece of the puzzle now falling into place. Kitty belonged behind that desk as much as I might have. She was part of the problem, not part of my solution. Jack must have known that all along.

I caught my reflection in the glass of a poster hanging on the wall. Undercover was an understatement. I pulled the cowboy hat off, only to expose matted hair that lacked its usual fluffy volume. Instead of running my fingers through it like instinct told me to do, I set the hat back on my head and tipped it forward to shield my eyes.

I walked past the front desk to the elevators, stopping for a second by marble table in the hallway. I picked up the squat ugly lamp and pulled the brown rubber electrical cord from the outlet. I wound the cord around my left wrist and pressed the call button, silently urging the elevator to get me out of there before anybody noticed what I'd done.

The elevator seemed to take an unbelievably long time to finally arrive, though it couldn't have been more than a minute.

The doors slid open and I got inside and jabbed the door close button repeatedly. I did not want company on this ride.

Just as the doors were about to slide closed, a hand fed between them, triggering the sensors. NO! The doors slowly retracted and my worst fear came true.

Brad stood in front of me.

I fumbled with the buttons on the control panel with my free hand as though I were searching for the one that would open the doors, all the while staring down, refusing to make eye contact. I accidentally hit the alarm button, sending a caustic ring through the shaft of the elevator well. The elevator didn't move. Brad stared at the lamp in my hands.

"Is that from the hotel?" he asked.

I looked at the lamp and nodded, the cowboy hat shielding most of my face.

"Most people take a bathrobe." He leaned into the elevator and pushed the alarm button, canceling the siren. He looked at the squat ugly lamp again. "Southwest design…I guess some people like it."

There were so many things I hadn't said to Brad at the top of that ski slope. I stared at the object, for fear if I looked at him I would say something I'd regret. Then Jack

Jordan, my savior Jack Jordan, appeared like an angel in the hallway. He stepped into the elevator between me and Brad

"Take the next elevator, man," he said.

"Excuse me?"

"The lady and I want to be alone."

"Sorry, man," said Brad, backing away from us into the lobby. The doors shut, leaving him on the outside and me on the inside with Jack.

"Was that your guy?"

"Yes."

He nodded once, then punched the 4 on the panel. "What's with the lamp?"

"What do you think is with the lamp?" I replied.

His face lit up as though it had been plugged into the now empty socket in the hallway.

I SPENT the last day of my vacation in the Carmel By-The-Sea Police Department surrounded by official looking men in black suits, white shirts, and skinny neckties. The only person in the room I recognized was Jack. He'd lied when he said he was head of security for the hotel. In reality, he was an FBI agent on the tail of a ring of jewel thieves.

The men and women behind the jewel smuggling had been working Carmel for months. It was a touristy town, a good place for outsiders to congregate, because everybody was an outsider, literally. They blended in by not blending in. The two men I encountered by the elevator the very first day were the men who anticipated going home with a fourteen-carat diamond from the Barbary Coast.

I answered a lot of questions and asked a few, too. I didn't get satisfactory answers. What I pieced together was the cops—the fake ones—had been planning a bait and switch all along. They knew the diamond was coming in to Carmel and the switch was happening at the hotel. Kitty worked for them, keeping lookout from the front desk. Her role allowed her access to the switchboard, to see what calls were going where. When Jack requested that no calls go through to my room, Kitty connected the dots. They didn't know how I figured into their overall plan, but my presence—and my reliance on the head of security—told them I was a part of it all. Once Kitty tipped them off, it wasn't difficult for them to keep tabs on me.

I asked if Louis and Gray Suit were the buyers, but they didn't tell me. I asked if the fake cops had been arrested and they didn't tell me that, either. I asked who had put the diamond in the lamp, when Jack had put the velvet pouch in my handbag, and if anybody knew how close they'd come to letting a team of decorators walk out of the building with a fourteen-carat diamond. I'd worked out a plausible explanation, but it was obvious nobody was going to validate my theory.

"Ms. Night, tell us why you refused to cooperate at first," said Jack.

"Mr. Jordan, with all due respect, nothing I've been told over the past four days made sense. I couldn't trust anybody."

"What changed?"

"It wasn't one thing, it was a bunch of things. Those men kept showing up and asking about me. And then you kept telling me they weren't asking about me, which I wanted to believe but couldn't. And then the phone calls started, and you told the receptionist to hold calls to my room, but when I called her back, she claimed she hadn't seen you since you returned from your vacation. You have to admit, from my perspective, things were very confusing."

"When did it click?"

"When I was at the diner, looking out the window at the hotel. I saw the van for the decorators and I realized why Brad was here. As soon as I realized you were telling the truth about him not being a guest at the hotel, I thought about everything else you'd told me. And once I determined everything you told me could be strung together as the truth, I realized everything else I'd been told had been a lie. From everybody. I knew I could trust you and nobody else. Not the cops. Not the operator. Not the men from the elevator."

"That's a big mental leap to make."

"It was more than that. Once I started looking around, I saw things that didn't make sense. One of the cops had long hair. I don't think police officers are allowed to wear their hair long. Their uniforms were wrong. I'd overheard Kitty talking to one of them, and realized she hadn't addressed him like she would a police officer, so she must have been involved."

"Not much gets past you, does it?" he said. I detected a complimentary tone, but I couldn't be sure.

"What do you mean?"

"Most people don't see that much of the world when they're on vacation."

"It's a compulsion. It's what I do."

"How's that?"

"I'm a decorator. I look at a room and I see what fits and what doesn't. I take away the problem and I'm left with the beginning of a solution."

"Is that how you figured out about the lamp?"

"I've hated that lamp since I first arrived. I saw it while waiting for the elevator after checking in. It's so out of place with the rest of the hotel. It didn't work, either. And once I realized the thing in the black pouch was a light bulb, I knew where to find the diamond. The lamp by the elevator was the perfect spot. Who looks at a lamp in a hotel? Nobody."

"You did."

"I already told you what I do." I stared at him for a couple of seconds, wondering if he expected me to continue or if he would keep pointing out that my brain didn't work like other people's brains.

"It didn't make sense that the decorators would leave the lamp. Especially Brad--he hates Southwest design! This would have been the first thing he replaced. Someone must have told him to leave it."

Jack checked some notes he'd made on a white lined tablet. Creases on his forehead deepened as he flipped back a couple of sheets, holding a black and gold ballpoint pen in one hand, touching different places on the paper as he scanned the contents. Four sheets back he tapped the paper a couple of times, looked at me, then looked back at the paper.

"You know this Brad guy pretty well, don't you?"

"I thought I did. Why?"

"I can't share anything from his statement with you."

"Meaning what? Did he say something about me? Did he recognize me?" I asked, leaning forward.

Jack didn't speak. Instead, his silence fell onto my questions. The longer they hung in the air, the more I regretted asking them.

"Never mind. I don't want to know."

Jack reached out and placed his hand on top of mine. "He said coming to this hotel was the second biggest mistake he'd made in his life."

I looked down at my hands, resting in my lap. "Did you look inside the lamp? Did you find it?"

"We did."

"And?"

"I can't tell you any more than that."

I understood.

I finished up with the men in the room and signed a piece of paper agreeing not to talk about what had happened during my vacation. When I was finished, I followed a uniformed officer out front where an attractive man with a light brown ponytail stood by the street. He wore a long-sleeved navy and white striped shirt and faded blue jeans that were stained with dirt at the knees. Next to him was a small, green, energy-efficient car.

"Are you Madison Night?"

"I am."

"I'm Merritt. Jack asked me to give you a ride back to the hotel."

I looked behind me to the police station where Jack Jordan stood framed out by the white brick archway that surrounded the front door. The keystone over his head looked like a crown. He smiled, nodded, and waved.

"Can you wait here for a second?" I asked Merritt. I walked back to the police station. Jack met me half way.

"Ms. Night, you're a heck of a woman. Forget about Turlington. I bet you'll find someone way better for you."

"What about you, Mr. Jordan? I seem to remember you had somebody who wouldn't appreciate you spending the night in my hotel room."

"I do." He put his hand on my upper arm and gently turned me to face the ponytailed man. "That's him."

And suddenly, the last mystery from my vacation in Carmel was solved.

EPILOGUE

When it came to Ms. Elliott Lisbon's suitcase, I was at a loss. Most of her belongings had been dirtied or destroyed. Everything, in fact, with the exception of the Dodgers T-shirt. I'd asked the hotel to launder the T-shirt for me. I wasn't sure how to explain the rest of the clothes, and, finally, I figured out a way to not explain them at all.

Dear Elliott,

I am not in the habit of opening stranger's luggage or using their personal belongings as my own, so it's with more than a little embarrassment I admit to having done just that. I can't explain why I did so, only that I had to, and I'm well aware of how thin that sounds. I'd tell you about the FBI and the investigation, but they told me I can't, so

I'll say the only thing I can. I'm sorry. I wish I could return your items in the condition they were in when I first opened your suitcase, but that's no longer an option. Since almost everything you had packed still had tags on it, I'm hoping it can be replaced. I'm also hoping this will cover it.

SINCERELY,

Madison Night

I CLIPPED ten one hundred dollar bills to the side of the paper and tri-folded it, then unfolded it and included another thousand dollars. I had no idea how much Elliott's items had cost her and since I lived in vintage sixties ensembles and dresses scored at flea markets and estate sales, I wasn't the go-to person for quoting the price of a new western ensemble. There had been a reward for my help in the capture of the jewel smugglers, and even though I wouldn't see the money right away, by now I trusted Jack Jordan enough to know it would arrive. Two thousand dollars would probably replace the contents of my entire closet if I didn't count my collection of hats, but somehow, when I considered the violation of Elliott Lisbon's personal belongings, two thousand dollars didn't seem like so much.

I printed the stranger's name in neat architectural drawing-like letters across the front of a crisp ivory envelope I'd bought at the local stationery store. I gently folded the T-shirt and set it in the middle of the suitcase.

Before putting the letter into the suitcase, I added a postscript:

PS: It might be fun to meet face to face sometime, but in the interest of full disclosure, you should know I'm a Phillies fan.

AFTERWORD

"Midnight Ice" was originally part of a novella collection entitled *Other People's Baggage.* The concept was the brainchild of three authors: Gigi Pandian, Kendel Lynn, and myself, dreamed up at Malice Domestic Fan Convention in 2012. *Wouldn't it be funny if our three different series characters got their luggage mixed up and had to each use items that weren't theirs to solve a mystery?* That was the jumping off point. Deadlines and word counts followed, and a draft of the book came shortly thereafter. It was one of the easiest and most fulfilling writing experiences I've ever had, made even more valuable by the participation of two authors I not only respect, but whose books I enjoy.

In a way, publishing this novella feels like Madison got her luggage back. If you'd like to find out how Elliott Lisbon solves a mystery using the contents of Jaya Jones' suitcase, you'll want to read "Switch Back." And for Jaya's use of

Madison's vintage belongings, read "Fool's Gold." Each prequel novella introduces our series characters in their unexpected and unplanned adventure. Like many unplanned adventures, this one was well worth the ride.

Read on for Chapter One of *Pillow Stalk*, Madison Night's first full adventure.

Xo,

   Diane

P.S. Sign up for The Weekly DiVa to receive news about girl talk, book talk, and life talk.

P.P.S. Please consider leaving a review for this book. No matter how brief or how long, reader reviews make a difference. Thank you!

P.P.P.S After writing this, I learned that Doris Day's Cypress Inn only has two floors. Que sera, sera!

PILLOW STALK EXCERPT

"Mr. Johnson, I would like to discuss to discuss the disposition of your mother's estate. I understand that you don't live around here—"

"Are you a lawyer?" asked a gruff voice on the other end of a crackly line.

"No, sir, I'm an interior decorator. Madison Night. I own Mad4Mod, on Greenville Avenue--"

"You're a decorator? You're calling me about my mom's tchotchkes?"

"I assure you that I mean no disrespect, but in my experience, you are about to be faced with the time consuming challenge of handling your mother's affairs, and I am in a position to take a portion of that challenge off your to-do list." Internally, I cringed at the holier-than-thou tone that had crept into my voice. It was a vocal knee-jerk reaction to people not taking me seriously. "It might interest you that I specialize in mid-century modern design."

"What was your name again? Madison?" he snapped. "What are you, twenty?"

I was used to people fixating on the least important detail of my phone call, my name. I pushed my long hair away from my face, then used my index finger to free a couple of strands that were stuck by my hairline, thanks to the Dallas-in-May humidity.

"Madison was my grandmother's maiden name," I offered, my head cradled in the kitschy yellow donut phone I used in the office. "I'm forty-seven, and I've been in this industry for over twenty years." The man was obviously more distraught over the death of his mother than the fact that my grandmother's surname had come into fashion sometime in the nineties, but at times like these, minor details could change the course of our conversation.

"My mom didn't have anything valuable. Her whole house was insured for fifteen thousand dollars, and I'd be better off if it had burned down and I got the check. Now I'm stuck with a bunch of junk I could never convince her to throw away."

I wrote fifteen thousand? on the side of a real estate flier that sat on my desk and put on my best can-do attitude. "Mr. Johnson, I'm prepared to make an offer on the entire estate. If you accept it, I can bring you a check tomorrow, and you can be on your way back to Cincinnati as soon as tomorrow night."

"Let me get this straight. You're offering to write me a check for stuff you haven't even seen?"

"That's correct."

"Lady, if this is a joke, you have a lousy sense of humor." He hung up on me.

I drummed my fingers against the top of my desk and stared at the flier, temporarily distracted by the overdone graphics and the photo of the woman listing houses. Pamela Ritter, a recently licensed real estate agent stared up at me, a picture of blonde hair and blue eyes not all that different than my own, though some twenty-years younger. Blast from the Past! screamed the heading, above listings for a string of ranch houses on Mockingbird. Live like a Mad Man! Promised the copy on the side. Turquoise bubbles filled the background of the paper, and starbursts, outlined in red, gave it a Pow! Bam! Bop! feel.

Pamela had jumped on the new movement to capitalize on all things fifties, thanks to a recent pop culture focus on the Eisenhower era. I'd been nurturing my passion for mid-century decorating since I was a teenager, since I first watched *Pillow Talk* after learning that I shared a birthday with an actress named Doris Day. I surrounded myself with items from the atomic age long before people like Pamela were born, and thanks to my business, I'd found others who shared my interest and appreciated my knowledge. I crumbled up the flier and tossed it at the trash bin. It bounced off the rim and landed on the carpet.

I glanced at the brushed gold starburst clock on the wall and twisted my blonde hair back into a chignon, then secured it with a vintage hairpin. It was ten minutes to six. I could leave early, I reasoned. Nothing was going to happen in ten minutes. I flipped the open sign to closed, locked the doors, and carried the small bag of trash out the back door, hitting the light switch on the way. I emptied the trash into the dumpster and rummaged through my handbag for my keys. That's why I didn't notice the flat tire.

I bent next to the tire and a slash of pain shot through my left knee. After a skiing accident two years ago, after fleeing down a mountain, I was left with a reminder that I had to look out for myself, because no one else would. The chronic pain forced me to acknowledge my limitations. It kept me from doing the kind of things that independent women knew how to do for themselves and Texas women took for granted. And today, it would keep me from getting home to Rock on time.

I went back inside the studio and called Hudson James, my handyman, though the term hardly described our relationship. "What are the chances you're up for rescuing a damsel in distress?" I asked.

"Depends on the damsel."

"I'm at the studio, and I've got a flat tire. I'd try to change it myself," I said, but stopped when the humiliating reality of me calling a man to ask for help resonated in my ears. I never thought I'd be that kind of woman.

"Madison, it's no problem. I'll be there in a couple of minutes."

Hudson's blue pickup truck pulled into the alley by my studio and parked next to the dumpster. His longish black hair had curled with the humidity, the front pushed to the side, behind his ear, the back flipping up against the collar of his t-shirt. "I thought you were calling because you had a job for me," he said.

I flushed. "I might," I said, "I'm still working it out. A woman died—"

He held up a hand. "I don't want to know the details."

"It's just business."

"I look at you and I see sweetness and innocence, not a ruthless business woman."

"Don't let the blonde hair and blue eyes fool you."

"Honey, they had me fooled me the first time I laid eyes on you." He winked and took the keys from my hand. Before he turned back to the car, his eyes swept over my body. "Is that a new dress?"

I looked down at my dress, a light blue fitted sheath dress that was significantly more wrinkled than it had been when I left the house this morning. A series of circles in gingham, stripe, and polka dot had been appliquéd to the neckline and hem.

"It's a new-old dress. Early sixties. From an estate sale in Pennsylvania, before I moved here. The woman died in a car accident—"

"Enough! I like the dress. I like the dress on you. But I don't need to hear the obituary of the woman who owned it first." He disappeared next to the tire.

"It's good for business," I said.

"The dress or the estate sales?"

"The only client I talked to today was over the phone, thank you very much." Maybe things would have gone differently if I had met Steve Johnson face to face. Not because of the dress, but because he'd see that I was legitimate.

Inside the studio, the phone jangled. Technically, Mad4Mod was still open, and even though I'd wanted to leave early, I didn't want to be one of those businesses that skimped on the hours. "Do you mind if I get that?"

"Nah, go ahead. This'll take a couple of minutes."

I picked up the ball of paper by the wastepaper basket and set it on the corner of my one-of-a-kind desk, then reached for the phone. "Mad for Mod, Madison Night speaking," I answered. I heard a click, then a dial tone. I sank into the chair and battled the crumpled up flier back and forth across the slick surface of the desk. It was a gift from Hudson, a hodgepodge of parts from items too damaged to repair. It had cost him more in time and vision than materials, and I wouldn't trade it for anything. More than once I'd asked him to be a partner in my business, and every time he declined. He was reliable, artistic, genuine, and best of all, smelled like wood shavings. In a parallel universe I might have entertained romantic thoughts of him, but life as it was for a single, forty-seven year old business woman with trust issues didn't allow for fantasies like that. And even if I was capable of giving in to attraction, I had long learned one lesson: men may come and go but good handymen last forever.

I closed up the studio for the second time. The phone mocked me from the other side of the back door. I ran back in and answered on the third ring, slightly breathless.

"Ms. Night, this is Steve Johnson. You called me about my mother's estate?" His voice had changed. The gruff had been traded for something else. Maybe the interest in my money. I seized the opportunity for a second chance.

"Mr. Johnson, I know it's unorthodox for me to have made an offer over the phone, but if you have time available tomorrow, I'd be more than happy to meet with you in person."

"That's not necessary. I changed my mind and I'm willing to sell. Call me at this number tomorrow and we'll wrap this thing up."

I grabbed a thick black marker out of the orange Tiki mug on the desk, flattened out Pamela's real estate flier, and scrawled the number across her smiling blonde face. "Perfect," I said, too eagerly, considering the circumstances. And then, for the second time that day, Steve Johnson hung up on me, leaving me to wonder what exactly had happened to change his mind.

ABOUT THE AUTHOR

Diane Vallere is a fashion industry veteran with a taste for murder. In addition to the Samantha Kidd Mysteries, she writes the Madison Night, Costume Shop, and Lefty Award-Nominated Material Witness series. She started her own detective agency at age ten and has maintained a passion for shoes, clues, and clothes ever since. For girl talk, book talk, and life talk, sign up for The Weekly DiVa at

https://dianevallere.com/weekly-diva.

Fly Me To The Moon

I'm Your Venus

Saturn Night Fever

Material Witness Mysteries:

Suede to Rest

Crushed Velvet

Silk Stalkings

Costume Shop Mystery Series:

A Disguise to Die For

Masking for Trouble

Dressed to Confess

Mermaid Mysteries:

Tails from the Deep

Murky Waters

Sleeping with the Fishes

Box Sets:

Messin' With The Kidd (Samantha Kidd Humorous Mysteries #1-3)

The Kidd Stays In The Picture (Samantha Kidd Humorous Mysteries #4-6)

Here's Lookin' At You, Kidd (Samantha Kidd Humorous Mysteries #7-9)

Sylvia Stryker Space Case Mysteries (Outer Space Mysteries #1-3)

Mermaid Mysteries (#1-3)

Non-Fiction:

Bonbons For Your Brain